Logan

Quentin

Kester

Leathers

Blizz

Li'l Sherman

Mr. Trout

Torch

Brian

THE YETI FILES

Meet the Bigfeet

KEVIN SHERRY

Library of Congress Control Number: 2014933337
ISBN: 978-0-545-55617-0

12 11 10 9 8 7 6 5 4 3 2 1   14 15 16 17 18 19/0

Printed in the U.S.A   23
First printing, October 2014

Designed by Jeannine Riske

THE YETI FILES

Meet the Bigfeet

KEVIN SHERRY

Scholastic Press / New York

Thanks to Teresa Kietlinski, Bill Stevenson, Nolen Strals, Ryan Patterson, Ed Schrader, Dina Kelberman, Alan Resnick, Ben O'Brien, Bob O'Brien, Dan Deacon, Eduardo Lino Costa, Emily Wexler, Matt Gemmell, the Black Cherry Puppet Theater, Baltimore, and especially to my huge awesome family and my parents.

For Brian

Chapter 1:
I'M A YETI

Hi there!
I'm Blizz Richards.
And I'm a yeti.
Nice to meet you!

What is a yeti, you ask?

Is a yeti a man?

Not quite.

Is a yeti an ape?

Nope.

2

This is a yeti;

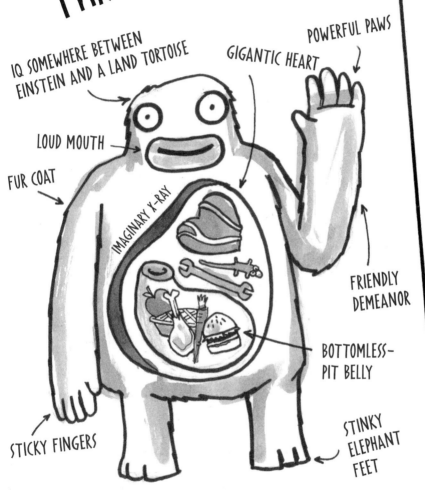

IQ SOMEWHERE BETWEEN EINSTEIN AND A LAND TORTOISE

POWERFUL PAWS

GIGANTIC HEART

LOUD MOUTH

FUR COAT

IMAGINARY X-RAY

FRIENDLY DEMEANOR

BOTTOMLESS-PIT BELLY

STICKY FINGERS

STINKY ELEPHANT FEET

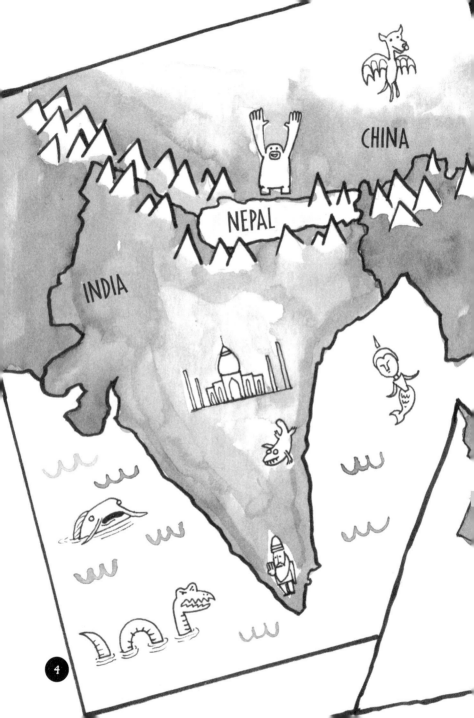

CHINA

NEPAL

INDIA

It's cold up here, so it's a good thing that I've got this nice fur coat. This is the entrance to my lair, my headquarters. I've got everything I need down here at HQ....

¼ SCALE MODEL, BLUE WHALE

UNDERWATER AIR LOCK

CRYPTO OATH

T. REX SKELETON

TIRE SWING

WORKSHOP

TRAMPOLINE

UNFINISHED
CHISELING PROJECT

MOVIE
THEATER

BRUCE LEE
THE BABOON

CRYSTAL
CAVE

ALL OF MY COMICS
AND BEST BOOKS

THINKING CHAIR

CRYPTOTRON

BLIZZ RICHARDS
SIGNED IN

RAT KING AT
TACO SHACK

JERSEY DEVIL - I
LOVE CANOEING

SUPERCOMPUTER

ROCK CLIMBING WALL

HOT TUB

I'm a yeti and that's a cryptid. A cryptid is a hidden animal whose existence has never been proven.

We have all
taken a powerful
oath to never be seen
by the outside world.
The secrecy keeps magic
and mystery in the minds
of humans. And we all know
how important that is.

Many different cryptids live all around the world.

And every one of us has taken the oath.

We try our best to honor it.

Chapter 2:
AN INVITATION

THE
BIG **FEET**
Family Reunion
WHERE? British Columbia, CANADA
WHEN? Just TWO DAYS!

I haven't gotten one of these in years!
Gather around, buddies.... We used to have these family reunions all the time... and boy, were they fun!

This handsome fellow's name is Brian. He's my cousin, but he's also a lot like my brother.

We grew up together.

Brian loves all animals.

He is super strong and
is a great cook.

INCREDIBLY POWERFUL TELESCOPE

HIGHLY POLISHED FIREMAN'S POLE

RATTLING DUNE BUGGY

ZIPPY ZIP LINE

BOUNCY TRAMPOLINE

COOKOUT CENTRAL

ORGANIC VEGETABLE GARDEN

We used to have a big party every year at Brian's awesome pad in Canada.

NETWORK OF LADDERS

VOLLEYBALL COURT

BUBBLING HOT TUB

EPIC TIRE SWING

BASKETBALL NET FOR SICK DUNKS

CHARBROIL SMOKER

But then Brian got **caught.**
Someone snapped his photo.

And soon the photo was everywhere.

Brian turned on his computer, and he saw that his picture was all over the entire Internet.

He was **mortified.** He had betrayed the cryptid oath. He couldn't bear to be seen ever again!

So Brian disappeared....

And it was all because of George Vanquist!

25

Chapter 3:
THE BAD GUY AND HIS DOG

ABOUNDING CONFIDENCE

George Vanquist

PRIZED MUSTACHE

CLUELESS

PISTACHIO

TROPHY TO HIMSELF

Noodles

146 IQ

GOOD SNIFFER

CARGO SHORTS

COST ANALYSIS OF LOST STRAWBERRY SCOOP

UNAPPRECIATED GENIUS

GEORGE VANQUIST
NEW BOOK

The photos George Vanquist took of Brian made George famous. He calls himself a cryptozoologist.

Ha!

"THE PHOTO"

BOOK
$20
SIGNED BOOK
$40

ME!

He tours for a living, doing school assemblies, motivational speeches, cocker spaniel conventions, and any other gig he can get.

Whoops!

Looks like a slide from my Jamaican vacation.

But he just doesn't get it!

Cryptozoology is not about fame at all. It's about the honor and secrecy of members. Cryptozoology is about retaining our magic, not about revealing us to the public!

He'll do anything to prove we exist.

And I'll do **anything** to thwart him.

Luckily, I've gotten good at thwarting ol' George.

Enough is enough.

George Vanquist has ruined things for our family for the last time. He's a weaselly little shrimp, and we are mighty Bigfeet, after all. And I've got a plan. We are going to find Brian and bring him to this reunion. It's time he got over all of this. And now that it's settled, there's one totally essential, very important thing we have to do.

Let's pack!

Chapter 4:
YETI GETS READY

BACK SCRATCHER

CASHEWS

NEWT

UKULELE

FIRECRACKERS

BUG NET

GRANOLA OAT BARS

DRAGON COMPASS

NOLEN

MEATBALL SUB

CURRENCY FROM TWENTY COUNTRIES

TIGHTY-WHITIES

Oh, excuse me, let me introduce you to my assistants and best buddies, Alexander and Gunthar.

CRYPTOTRON

GUNTHAR
signed in

MERMAN
what is rain?

ABRA

EVIL
yum!

RALPH

O'BRIEN

Hi, I'm Alexander.

I work for Santa for four months a year. It's so **stressful,** Santa gives us an eight-month vacation.

But I **love** working, so in my time off, I work with Blizz. Our missions are the **most fun ever,** which is saying a lot since my other job is at the North Pole.

CRYPTOT

cats on the

AUG

It's all right, I guess.

Hey, Alex!

FTING!

Boink! Oww!
Hey, quit it! And my name is Alexander, not Alex!

ACTUALLY, THIS JOB IS AWESOME!

39

Last but **certainly** not least, my faithful hound, Frank the Arctic fox. He's got a lot of tricks up his sleeve.

BRITISH
COLUMBIA

CANADA
AMERICA

NEVADA

Okay, so I'm all packed and ready to go.
Now it's time to head to Canada!
But we are going to need transportation.

I know just who to call!

FLY GUY

CALL

But have you ever flown to Canada with a **1,200-pound** yeti on your back?

Chapter 5:
ARRIVING IN CANADA

See you later, Blizz. Thanks for the generous burrito gift card. Call me anytime!

You're welcome, Jack! You've earned it!

Meanwhile...

...Frank slipped away...

...on urgent business.

NO BRIAN ANYWHERE!!!

ROOF FULL
OF HOLES

CRUMBLED COURT

GNARLED
NET

Let me introduce you to my family. This is Marlon the skunk ape and that is Timmy the Sasquatch.

I'm sitting on a rock under a tree re-reading Harry Potter Book Six. It's a one-person job. Leave me alone. —

But who sent the invitation?

Of course! Grandfather Goatman!

It was you, wasn't it, Grandpa?! I could tell it was your handwriting.

Yup, guilty!

So many of my best memories are from those reunions. But it won't be the same without Brian. I sure hope we can find him. Bigfeet, it's time to track him down!

Well, this might be a clue. It's a

"big" footprint

and a sprig of wild rosemary.
Brian has big feet and
loves to cook savory dishes.
We're on the right track, guys!

*The Bigfeet don't know it, but not so
very far away, trouble is brewing....*

Chapter 6:
VANQUIST IN CANADA

George Vanquist here.

Richest and most famous

cryptozoologist in the world. Believe it or not, some people are still skeptical that Bigfoot exists, so I'm back here to get even more proof.

And to ensure my success I've brought...

a state-of-the-art rocket bus...

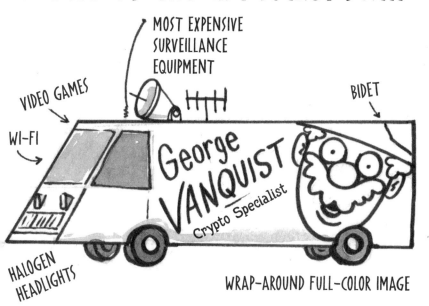

MOST EXPENSIVE
SURVEILLANCE
EQUIPMENT

VIDEO GAMES

BIDET

WI-FI

George VANQUIST
Crypto Specialist

HALOGEN
HEADLIGHTS

WRAP-AROUND FULL-COLOR IMAGE

and Eagle Eye Z5000.

700 MEGAPIXELS

HD VIDEO
TOUCHSCREEN

MACRO
LENS

18.6MP DIGITAL SLR
DOUBLE-ZOOM LENS

NOODLES! What in the world is all this? Maps, maps, maps... **you know I hate maps!**

Can't you just get me where I need to go without them?
Do I have to do everything myself?
Are you man's worst friend?

Wait! I never even learned how to drive.
I CAN'T DRIVE!

I have to get Bigfoot, I just *have* to!

Heh heh heh...

Chapter 7:
FIND BRIAN

Meanwhile, the Bigfeet are also still looking for Brian.

These Canadian woods go on forever! He could be **anywhere!**

65

We've been looking forever!

Not here.

Not in this cave.

Do you know where?

BRIAN! It's you, you ol' Bigfoot! And you're roasting red potatoes with olive oil and rosemary. But I don't think you made enough to go around....

HOLY COW!

It's my whole family! You all probably hate me for getting caught and letting our secret out.

Brian, it wasn't your fault. It was an accident. We've all missed you so much. We love you, Bigfoot. Now that we've found you, let the family reunion begin!

We've got games, grub, and good times ahead. Let's party like the crazy cryptids we are!

Alexander and Gunthar, I need you to stand guard. Look out for **sneaky photographers** who may try to take our picture. Here are some binoculars to help you spot them. REMEMBER, no one can find us. I'm counting on you guys to keep our secret safe and sound!

71

NO! Blizz gave them to meee!

Err... come on, let me see.

Stop it, Gunthar. They're mine!

I just want to try them. Stop hogging!

OW! Hey, quit it!

You broke them!

Look what you did!
How are we going to keep a lookout now?

Ugh, and get your feet
out of my face!

What's wrong with my feet?

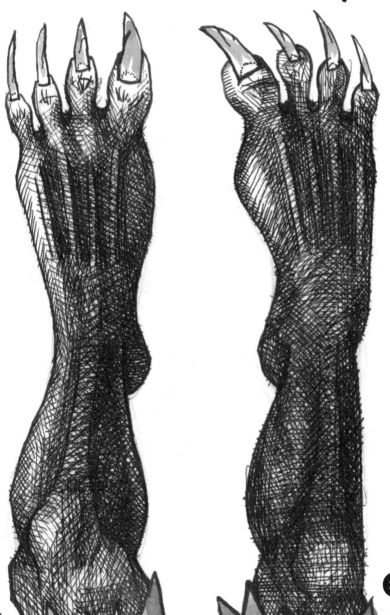

And later still...
... so Blizz stepped on the dragon's tail, but we got out in time!
I'm glad we met. Wanna go to a party?
It's just across the road.
George VANGST
Look who it is... Blizz isn't going to like this...

While Alexander and Gunthar are fighting, and Frank is making a new friend, Blizz and the family are partying hard. Too bad no one is watching out for rogue cryptozoologists with bad intentions.

78

Chapter 8:
VANQUIST'S PROOF

Well, hello there.
I've successfully navigated us to British Columbia, Canada, to uncover the Bigfoot. No thanks to Noodles.

BEEP BEEP BEEP!

PARKING PERFECTLY

And I will not fail. I will get undeniable proof of Bigfoot. Now I just have to find him! Let's go. I know a shortcut....

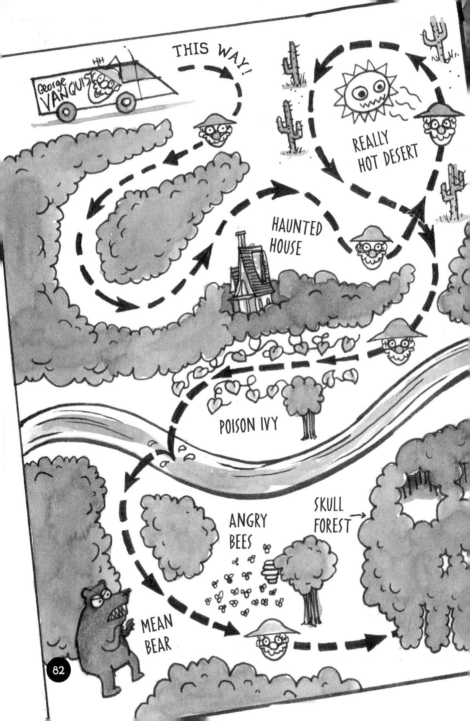

Did you like that, Noodles?
Leading me the wrong way to make a fool of me?

I know you think I'll never find Bigfoot again. And I've been patient with your fumbling so far. But if you don't shape up, your kind owner might not be so kind anymore.

Chapter 9:
DISCOVERED

OMG!

This is my big opportunity!

You were wrong. Noodles, you were wrong! I was right. I am the winner. You doubted me, Noodles. Shame on you!

Shame on you! You are one big dummy.
Now the world will have to agree that I'm
THE WORLD'S BEST CRYPTOZOOLOGIST!

I DID IT! I DID IT!

And once I download the photos to my system, the whole world will know I was right. In fact, I'm going to call every reporter and TV anchorwoman I know right now, and give them the *scoop!*

That guy seems really **nasty.**
You know, you don't have to put up
with that kind of treatment!

Yeah! No one should be treated like
that. And you seem like a cool guy.
What's your name?

93

Can I please have that camera?

This thing? Please take it. I'm not helping George anymore. He's on his own!

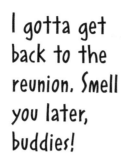

I gotta get back to the reunion. Smell you later, buddies!

C'mon, Noodles. I think I know what to do to help you escape that awful owner of yours!

Channel Six? Have I got a story for you! I have proof that Bigfoot lives.... What? No, this isn't a prank call! Can you hold on a minute?

Noodles, get your lazy dog butt in the cryptomobile! We need to get back to my cryptolab ASAP!

Chapter 10:
FRANK'S FINE FETCH

While George zooms away in the cryptomobile, Frank arrives at the reunion with a gift for Blizz.

It's a tie!

Guess we'll settle this next year.

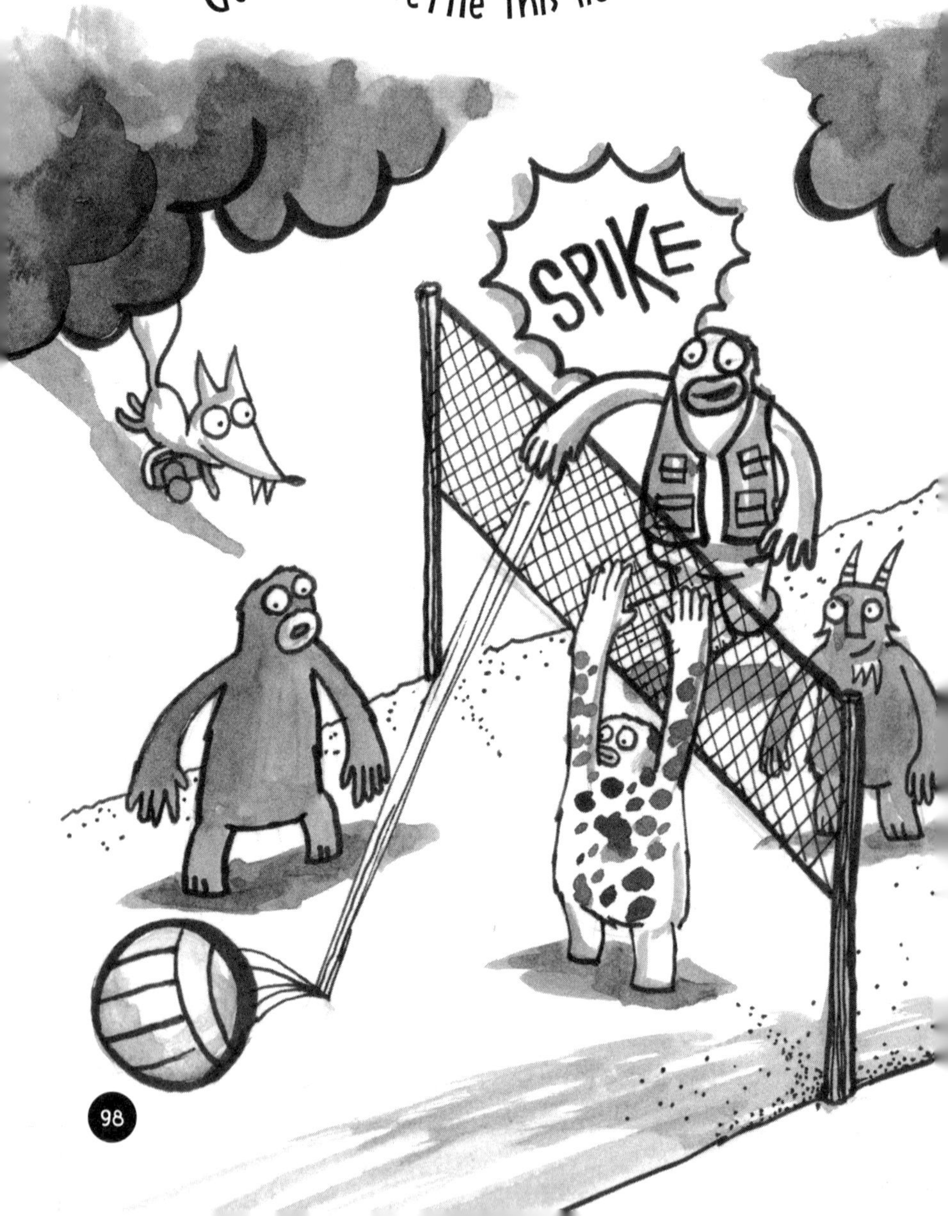

Oh, hey, Frank! Who's a good boy?
Whatcha got here? Is it a camera?
It's a camera!

"Property of George Vanquist"? How did he get these shots? Did anyone else spot us? Alexander and Gunthar, do you know anything about this?

Chapter 10 ½:
VANQUIST TAKES A WRONG TURN

Hmm ... we seem to be in some sort of desert.
Beautiful, though. I think I'll take a picture.
Let me get my camera.

It's not here. I lost it.

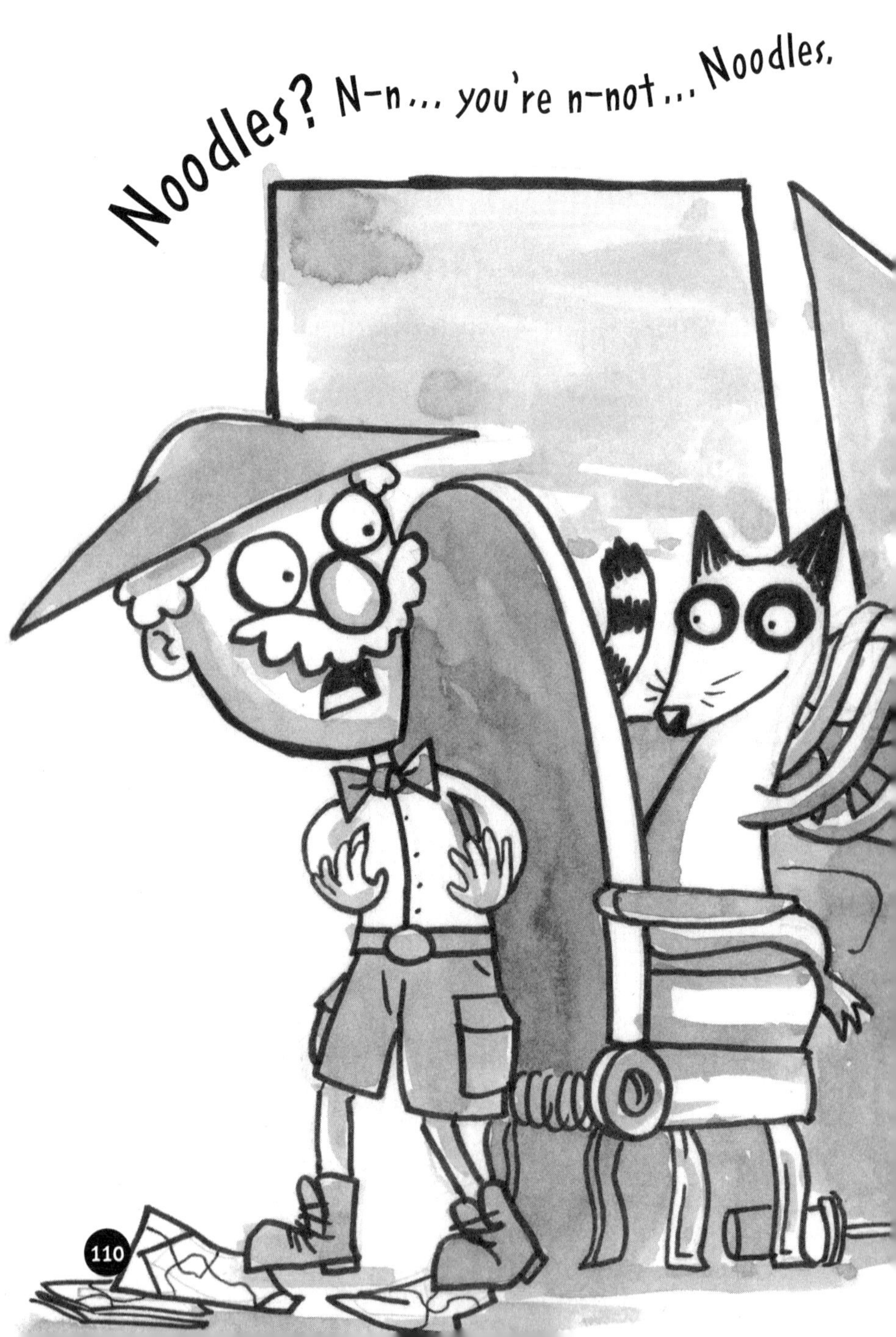
Noodles? N-n... you're n-not... Noodles.

Where am I? Who am I? Who are you?
Why are we here? What is the meaning of
life? Why is the sky blue? And why are those
birds staring at me? Do they have my camera?

Chapter 11:
BACK AT HQ

Wow! I had a great time at the reunion. But it sure is nice to be home again. And I could use a long nap.

HOT DOG WITH COLESLAW

TROY THE ROBOT

ANCIENT ALIEN SKULL

TIME FOR ANOTHER ADVENTURE!

LOCH NESS MONSTER

A.K.A. NESSIE
HABITAT: Scotland
LIKES: honesty and privacy
DISLIKES: jerks and cars

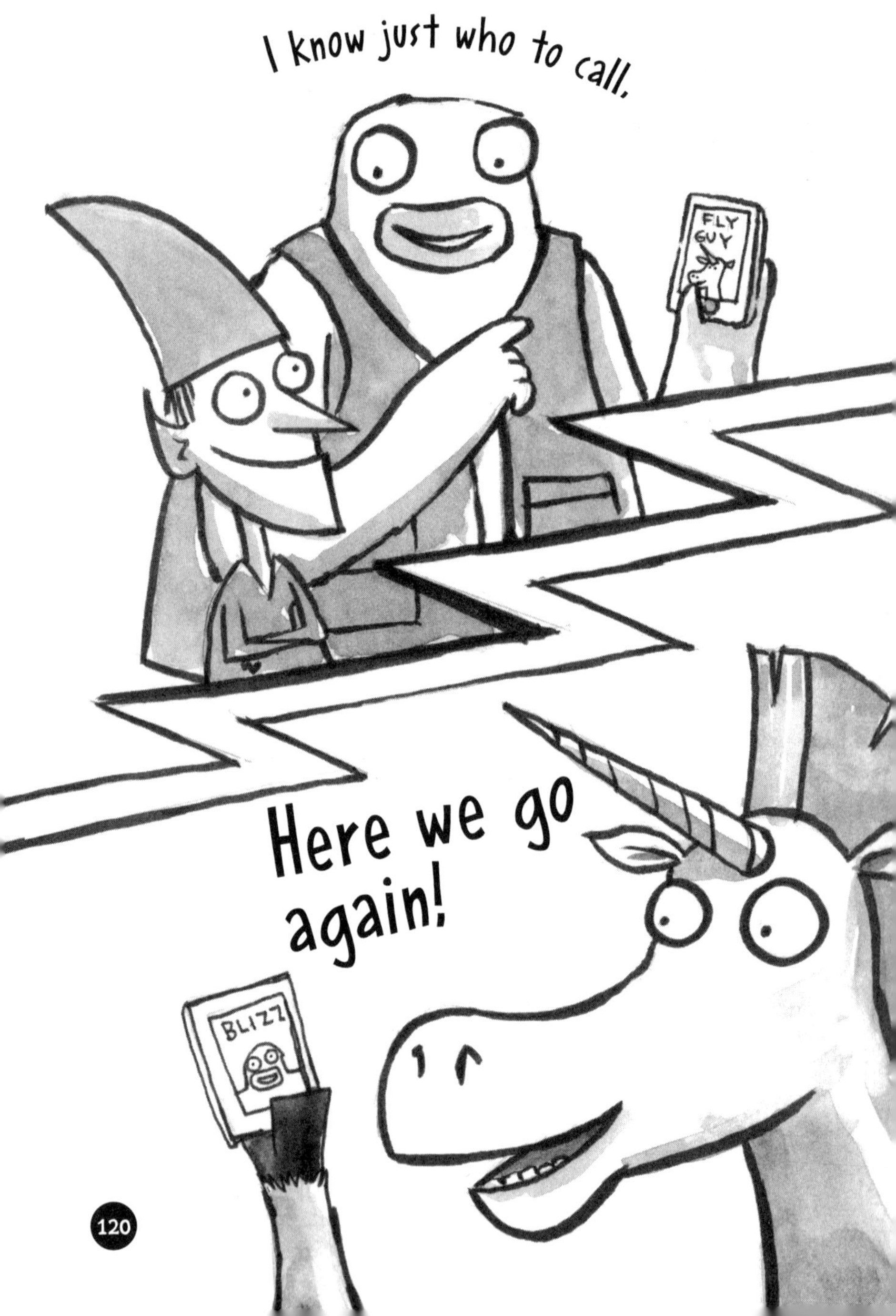
I know just who to call.
FLY GUY
Here we go again!
BLIZZ

But first, we would like to welcome a new member to our team.